Six Stories of Hearts
Bound in Dark
and Blood

A SHADOW OF LOVE

SHIRLEY SIATON

A SHADOW OF LOVE
Six Stories of Hearts Bound in Dark and Blood

ISBN 978-1-961052-23-9 (**paperback,** *romance)*
ISBN 978-621-490-130-2 (**paperback,** *discreet)*

1st Edition, September 2025

Published by Shirley S. Parabia
Romance cover by Artista Gráfico Design
Discreet cover by RJ Creatives Design Services
Interior formatting by Champagne Book Design

Inky Sword Book Publishing
Barangay Quezon, Arevalo, Iloilo City 5000
Republic of the Philippines
inkysword.com

A NOTE FOR THE READER

Welcome to the world of *A Shadow of Love*. The six stories contained in this collection are an exploration of love in its most raw, dangerous, and desperate forms. They are, by nature, intended for a **mature audience** and delve into intense and often dark themes.

This section is provided to help you make an informed decision about whether this collection is the right read for you at this time. The following list details some of the sensitive topics and potential triggers contained within these pages. Please be aware that this list may contain minor spoilers.

Your well-being as a reader is important. Please proceed with care. ♥

CONTENT WARNINGS

This collection contains depictions and discussions of the following:

Graphic Violence & Death: Including gang-related violence, kidnapping, assassination, physical altercations, and on-page character death.

Explicit Sexual Content: Including consensual, on-page sexual scenes. Some scenarios involve power imbalances (e.g., captor/captive) that may be challenging for some readers.

Abuse & Trauma: Including references to and confrontations with past physical, emotional, and familial abuse.

Mental Health: Including themes and depictions of anxiety, depression, grief, panic attacks, and PTSD.

Other Mature Themes: Including criminal activity and drug/alcohol use.

To all my dark romance readers

This is my gift to you

CONTENTS

A SHADOW OF LOVE

THE BOY AND
THE SKY

CHAPTER 1

The Sky

I'VE PROBABLY LOOKED UP AT THE SKY A HUNDRED TIMES in the last hour.

Maybe more.

It's one of those nights where the sky feels too big, too clear. The constellations are showing off. Even the North Star shines steady and bright like it knows what it's doing.

The moon is full, a perfect white coin cut into the dark. It glows as if it's lit from within by all the fireworks and promises of the New Year.

But I can't enjoy it.

I drop my gaze back down to the street, to the sidewalk beneath my feet. The stone is cold and chipped in places. I'm sitting on a freshly painted bench at the corner of my favorite intersection, the one near the old convenience store and the ice cream shop that still plays OPM love songs from the early 2000s.

Neon signs from every direction bathe the pavement in a chaotic kaleidoscope of red, green, yellow, orange, and blue. It should feel festive. Comforting.

It doesn't.

The pavement's stained with old gum and littered with newspapers and flyers, half-wilted in the night air. There's graffiti on the wall behind me, something angry in red spray paint I stopped trying to read twenty minutes ago.

I look up again.

And suddenly, the sky looks different.

Clouds have crept in where stars used to be. The moon's gone blurry. The blue-black canvas is turning the color of dust.

It feels like the universe is folding in on itself. Like even the stars are sick of waiting.

Like me.

I pull my legs up and rest my chin on my knees. It's been nearly two hours since I got here. Almost half a day since I said yes to Fidel's call, since I got way too excited for someone who's never even noticed me in school before.

He'd asked me to join him at the cinema. Me.

And I'd said yes so fast I could have choked on the word.

I'd dressed up—my best green sundress, the soft white cardigan I've been saving since Christmas, the pair of flats I begged my mother to buy last payday. I even raided her dresser for a touch of blush and one tiny spray of her best perfume. I looked in the mirror and thought, for once, I looked pretty.

I wanted to believe I was wanted.

And now? I'm not just alone. I'm humiliated.

He stood me up.

That scumbag Fidel stood me up.

The clock on my phone blinks mockingly. It's already 8:42 PM. He was supposed to pick me at 7:00.

I huddle deeper into my cardigan, gripping it so hard the fabric bunches at my elbows. If I had a cord in my hands, I'd wrap it around his neck and pull tight until he felt even a shred of what I feel now.

I swear, smoke's coming out of my nose.

Puff. Puff. Puff.

Damn it.

Damn him.

"Stood you up, hasn't he? Been two hours. Almost."

I jump, heart slamming against my ribcage. My body goes rigid, like I've just been caught doing something I shouldn't.

The voice comes from behind the bench.

I twist around on reflex, fists half-raised even though I've never thrown a punch in my life.

There, half-shadowed beneath the awning of the ice cream shop, is a boy. Maybe a young man. I can't really tell.

He looks like someone who doesn't belong anywhere. He's wearing a tattered hoodie and loose jeans, with a knit cap pulled low over a head of wild dark curls. He's leaning against the wall like the night belongs to him.

"Who the hell are you?" I blurt out, voice more shrill than strong.

He steps into the light and smiles—white teeth, easy grin. He looks…around my age. Maybe a little older. His eyes are deep and dark. His skin is rich brown and sun-kissed, and despite the ragged clothes, there's something solid and effortless in the way he stands.

He stands as if he knows himself. As if he's not ashamed of anything.

My goodness, he's cute. For lack of a better word.

"I'm Adam," he says, sounding like we're at a party in an expensive restaurant across the city.

I don't answer. I flop back onto the bench and cross my arms, trying not to look at him again.

But of course he slides onto the bench, right next to me.

I feel the wood groan slightly under his weight. I glance sideways. Up close, he's even more striking. There's something sharp and worldly about his features, something almost foreign. His eyes tilt up just a little at the corners, and his jawline is criminally unfair.

He's way too attractive for someone wearing a sweatshirt full of holes.

"What's your name?" he asks.

I sigh, still staring at the road. "Skye."

"Nice." He holds out a paper cup. Steam rises from the lid. "Want some? Coffee. Manang Menchie's best."

The smell wafts toward me. There's a hint of something chocolatey in it.

I usually hate when people assume I want to share space. But there's no arrogance in his offer. No smooth lines. Just... warmth.

I almost say yes.

"It smells good," I admit. "But no. Thanks, though."

He nods and sips. Silence settles between us again. Strangely, it's not awkward. Just quiet.

I peek at his clothes again. They really are too thin for this weather.

"It's freezing," I say before I can stop myself. "Aren't you cold?"

He shrugs. "I'm used to it."

His tone is soft. Not pitying. Just factual.

Then he looks at me again, and this time, there's something playful in his eyes.

"Your boy Fidel's not coming, you know."

The name hits like a slap.

My eyes narrow. "How do you know his name?"

Another shrug. "I know people. He's friends with some of the guys around here. Buys weed pretty often."

I stare at him.

No. Not Fidel.

Not Mr. MVP, Not Mr. Popularity, the golden boy of our school. He couldn't be...

Except I've heard the rumors. We all have. I just didn't want to believe them.

I open my mouth to argue, to say something cutting. But the words die in my throat.

Adam's already looking away. "You're not the first girl he's done this to. Same spot. Same move. It's almost predictable, in a way."

I blink hard, still suspended in disbelief. "You're kidding."

"I wish." He lets out a slow breath. "There was this one girl. Came back twice. The second time, she screamed at me. Thought I was stalking her and threatened to call the cops on me. All I did was try to help."

His voice cracks slightly on that last word.

I don't know what to say. The anger that's been boiling in my chest starts to soften.

We talk, slowly. Cautiously.

He tells me he left home years ago. He couldn't stand the beatings from his stepdad. Or the way his mother took her new husband's side all the time and blamed him instead.

He's been moving around ever since. Taking odd jobs. Never touching drugs. Never selling. Never running.

I believe him.

I tell him about college. About not being smart or pretty or popular to get any attention. About just being enough to get by without getting really chosen for anything.

He believes me.

It's getting late. I can feel it in my bones, in the weight of the sky pressing down.

Adam stands, stretching a little, and glances at me. "Bet they're worried about you at home."

I hesitate, then nod.

"I'll walk you," he offers. "If that's okay."

There's no pressure in his voice. Just the offer.

And something in me makes me say yes.

So I rise and fall into step beside him.

People look. Of course they do. I'm a girl in a nice dress, walking down the street with a guy who looks like he sleeps in alleys and on rooftops.

But I don't care.

Because for the first time tonight, I don't feel like someone discarded.

I feel seen.

And maybe, as we walk away from that corner under the faded lights and dying stars…

I feel like I've been chosen.

Like the real night is only just beginning.

CHAPTER 2

The Boy

Iт's two days later when I return to the bench after class.

I tell myself it's just on the way. Just a passing thought.

But the truth is, I'm hoping.

Hoping I'll see him again. Hoping I'll get to say hello. Maybe say thank you for seeing me home safely.

Maybe even buy him an ice cream, or some fishball.

But the bench is empty.

I wait for a while, pretending not to. I watch the sky again as if it might offer answers.

Then I ask around, quietly and carefully. I talk to the vendors, the old woman selling peanuts, the cigarette man with the toothy smile, even the ones lurking in the shadows of the alley.

"Adam?" I ask. "Do you know someone named Adam?"

They all shake their heads. Some don't even look up. No one knows who I'm talking about.

It's like he was never here at all.

I come back again. And again.

Even when I say I won't.

Even when I know better.

I wait through sundowns and streetlights. Through cold breezes and humid silences.

But he never comes.

I never see him again.

And yet, sometimes, when I pass by the intersection and the lights catch just right, I swear I still feel him beside me.

A ghost made of kindness.

A boy made of starlight who vanished into the city's smoke.

And maybe he was never lost.

Just passing through.

Just in time to choose me, in that one night under the glowing sky.

THE GIRL WITH THE ALMOND EYES

CHAPTER 1

The Green Umbrella

I WAS FOURTEEN THE FIRST TIME I SAW HER.

She was standing beneath the awning outside our school's administration building, holding a green umbrella speckled with cartoon frogs. Her uniform was soaked at the hem, her shoes ruined by the heavy rain, but she looked like summer anyway.

She had long black hair, wind-kissed cheeks, and a smile like sunlight breaking through clouds.

She smiled at me, almost gently. Her almond eyes took in the soaked version of me like someone who actually mattered.

"You look like you need this," she said, offering me her umbrella, moving over to make room for me.

I didn't take it.

Instead, I memorized the shape of her fingers on the curved plastic handle, the way her wet hair clung to her cheek, the rhythm of her voice.

I wrote about her that night.

It was a poem, I realized later on. My first one.

She never knew.

Her name was Mireya.

She lived in a small white house with potted daisies on the windowsill, while I lived two blocks over, in a place that never smelled like anything but old rust and rain that never dries.

People called me Niko.

The boy with the busted life and even more busted shoes. My father was in prison. My mother didn't come home unless she had to; she lived in bingo halls and at mahjong tables instead.

I saw her every day in school. She liked to sit beneath the fire escape behind the cafeteria and read. Sometimes I pretended to smoke just so I could sit near her. She'd wrinkle her nose and say, "That'll kill you, you know."

I shrugged. "So will living."

She never laughed at that. She'd just glance at me with those almond eyes and say, "Don't make dying your ambition."

I didn't know how to tell her it already was.

I watched her from the corners of hallways, the back of classrooms I snuck into just to see her.

She always noticed people, even the invisible ones. She talked to me sometimes. She once gave me a stick of banana cue when I had nothing to eat. She even laughed at a joke I didn't mean to say out loud.

She was kind. Unshakably, stupidly kind.

Mireya didn't belong in my world.

But she lived in my poetry.

I started writing because of her. I hid my poems in notebooks and later, when I joined the gang, in scraps of receipt paper and cigarette boxes.

I never gave her one. I never had the guts. But I wrote like I was bleeding ink. Like every line might save me.

When we were seventeen, she gave me a Band-Aid. I had a broken lip and a bruised eye from a fight I didn't win, and she pressed it into my hand like it was a treasure.

"You don't have to keep doing this, Niko," she said.

But I did. For my brothers who were my only real family. For the streets of De la Rama. For the ones who would die if I didn't hold the line.

Life caught up with me, as it always does.

My father died in a riot at the provincial jail. My mother's lungs gave up on her and the cigarettes she loved more than me.

I didn't go to college. I joined the Marilas, made it a

full-time job. Not because I wanted to. Because I had to. We were the ones who kept order at the docks. We were monsters, but we were family.

And still I wrote.

In ink and shadows, in blood and silence. I wrote her name in letters I never sent. Wrote apologies I could never give. Wrote confessions I never had the courage to say.

Wrote about another life, one where I could actually stand under the frog umbrella with the almond-eyed girl of my dreams.

She stayed in the city and became a nurse.

She always helped out in our neighborhood, smiling at those who came in pain, in need, and in desperation. Once, I saw her patch up a teenaged boy who got shot in a turf fight. No questions asked, even when she saw our colors.

She looked at me then.

"Niko," she said. "You look tired. Do you need anything?"

She spoke without fear. Without judgment.

I couldn't even answer.

I left before I did something stupid.

We crossed paths again and again. At the public market. A church pew. A wake for someone we both knew. She always said hi. I always froze.

My brothers laughed and said she was too good for me. I agreed.

But I wrote her another poem.

CHAPTER 2

The Black Coffee

ONE NIGHT, I SAW HER IN AN ALL-HOURS COFFEE SHOP near the river. She wore her hair in a braid, and her white uniform was rumpled from what must have been a long shift.

I asked for two black coffees from the counter. I didn't realize my own hands were trembling as the barista handed me the change.

I went to the tiny two-seat table she had settled on outdoors.

"May I join you?" I asked as I put one of the red cardboard cups in front of her.

She looked up, not surprised at all to see me. She only nodded.

Her almond eyes took me in closely as I settled on the stool across hers.

"You look…" she began, but trailed off.

I waited.

"You still look tired, Niko."

I gave her a smile that didn't reach anything. "You remembered me. And my name."

"I remember everything."

I wanted to say it then, more than anything.

Then why didn't you see I was always yours?

But I didn't.

I finished my coffee without saying another word, but I left something on the table, in the space between our red cups.

It's one of my old poems written on the inside of a cigarette box.

She didn't say anything.

I didn't look back.

The war came fast.

Turf was turf. Blood was blood. De la Rama was ours, even if the Valientes didn't agree.

We lost three boys in one week.

I told myself I was doing it for the family. But in my darkest moments, when I stood in the rain with my hands still shaking from the blade or the gun or the weight of the choice, I thought of her.

The girl with the almond eyes who once told me to live.

I didn't expect the bullet. No one ever does.

It tore through my side like fire.

I bled out in the alley behind the videoke bar, beneath a flickering light and the eyes of the patron saint of voyages painted on the dock walls.

My phone buzzed once. It was a message I'd scheduled to send at nine in the evening.

To her.

Somehow, I knew tonight was going to be it.

The message just had three lines:

You were my sun.

You were the only thing that made me write.

I hope you smile when you think of me.

I closed my eyes thinking of her hands. Of the Band-Aid and the banana cue.

Of the green umbrella with the frogs.

Of the moments she always said my name like it meant something more than just a boy life threw to the wind without a second thought.

I thought of her first words to me.

"You look like you need this."

This time, I answered. Because I knew this was my last chance.

Yes, Mireya. I need you.

I love you. I always will.

Maybe, in another life, I would have joined her under the umbrella, in the space she made for me.

Maybe, then, I would have made her mine.

But in this one…

She was the only poem I ever finished.

CHAPTER 3

The Red Bag

H E DIES ON A THURSDAY.

I didn't understand the message I got from him that night, but I do now.

I find out on a Saturday, when a man with eyes like steel and tattoos like maps knocks on our gate at almost midnight.

He's terrifying, tall and built like a tank, wearing a nondescript black shirt and faded camouflage pants. He doesn't speak at first. He just stares at me.

Then he hands me a red reusable bag. As I take it with trembling hands, I hear pieces of paper and cardboard scrunching against each other.

"I'm Mart Marila," he says at last. "Niko's brother."

I nod, swallowing hard, too afraid to blink.

"He wrote these for you," he says, voice low, like it hurts

to speak. He tilts his head at the bag. "We found them with his things."

He doesn't stay. He nods once and disappears into the night like a shadow.

I lock up and go inside the house. I sit on the sofa and pour out the bag's contents onto the low table.

Inside are poems. Dozens of them, maybe even more than a hundred. All scribbled onto torn cardboard packaging or oddly shaped sheets of paper.

Some of them are half-finished, some torn, all bleeding with longing. My name is in every one.

So is the name of the boy with the bruised knuckles and tired, sad eyes. The boy I always noticed. The boy I always wanted to save.

The boy I wanted to give my heart to, but never let me in.

I sit and read until the sun comes up.

I cry like I never cried before.

And when I finish the last one, I kiss the piece of cardboard, the one where Niko had doodled a girl with an umbrella surrounded by frogs and hearts.

I kiss the words he had written in red ink.

You were my first warmth.

You were the only good thing I never touched, the dream I never deserved, the sun I watched rise from a rooftop, knowing I would always belong to the night.

I wrote you poems you'll never read.

You smiled at me like I wasn't lost.

You looked at me like I mattered.

I think that's what saved me for as long as it did.

And I'm sorry.

I'm sorry I couldn't be better. Sorry I never told you.

I wish I could see you one last time. I wish you could read this. I wish you could have known.

I loved you.

I loved you more than any of them will ever understand.

I hope you never forget to carry your umbrella.

It's raining again.

And I remember everything about you.

~ Niko

And I whisper into the bleeding dawn, "I remember everything, too, Niko."

A SHADOW HEART

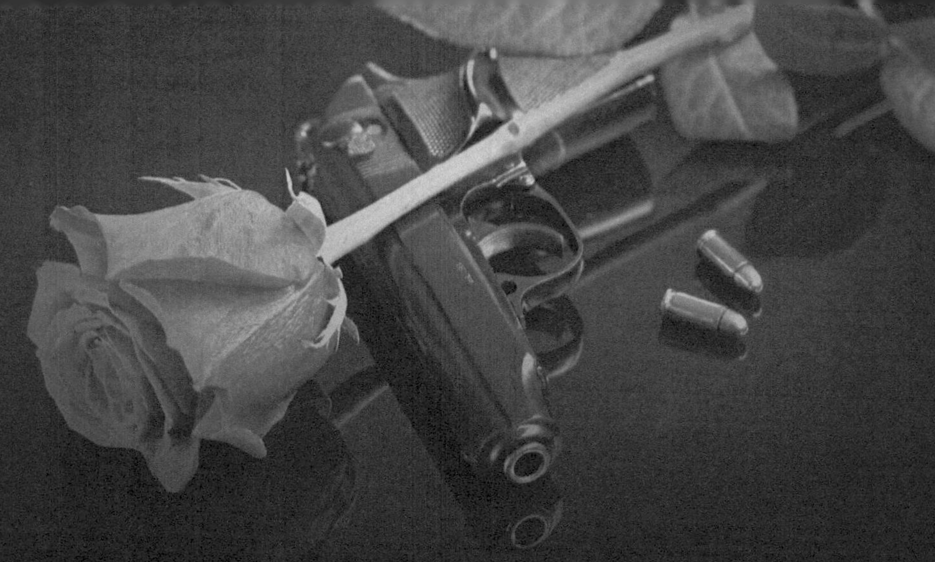

CHAPTER 1

The Lights

THE LIGHTS ARE TOO BRIGHT.

Not the kind I'm used to—neon signs flickering in seedy motels, or the sterile glow of Makati towers.

These are cheap, borrowed bulbs strung across bamboo poles, their wires sagging, their glow uneven. But it works. The coffee shop looks alive.

Music spills out into the street, a mix of OPM classics and whatever upbeat trash the DJ they hired could cobble together. The banner above the little shop reads *Brew & Break: Coffee for the Puyat Generation.*

It's all clever. And true.

I know I shouldn't be here, but I am.

The job offer hasn't come in yet. No contract. No instructions.

I'm only here to watch. To learn. That's what I tell myself. But my eyes keep finding her.

Lara Bienvenides. A politician's daughter. A Congressman's pretty little gem. She shouldn't normally be anywhere near this crowd. The coffee shop is filled with a mix of students in uniforms, call center kids still in ID lanyards, and yuppies clutching cheap plastic tumblers like trophies.

But here she is, with her older brother Luke. He owns the place and she works for him. It's not a secret that they have left their parents to strike out on their own. Their father, Lawrence, had been implicated one too many times in misspent pork barrel investigations and disappearing flood control projects, but he's slipped out all of them fairly unscathed.

Lara has the sleeves of her simple white shirt rolled up. Her hair's tied back, a few strands sticking to her forehead with sweat. She's carrying trays of iced coffee and complimentary cookies, laughing with strangers, brushing errant sugar and crumbs off her jeans as moves around the room.

She looks free.

And it makes something twist in my chest.

A group of young men and women invite me to join their table, but I ignore them. I'm leaning against the far wall, shadowed, my usual place wherever I am. I sip the cold bottle of light beer I bought just to blend in.

My mask is off. Not the cloth one, but the mask of distance. Tonight, I let myself watch.

Later, Luke makes a speech. It's nervous and awkward, about dreams and hard work and no shortcuts. The crowd cheers him on. Lara claps the loudest. Her smile is proud, fond, and real.

It doesn't take long before couples take to the tiny space in the middle of the shop, set up as a makeshift dance floor.

Then the music changes to something slow, almost moody. An old Rivermaya song, maybe.

Before I know what I'm doing, I push off the wall.

Lara's near the counter, wiping away sweat from her forehead with a white handkerchief, a small smile of relief on her delicate face. She looks up, startled, when I stop in front of her.

My voice comes out low and steady. Not a request. Not quite a command.

"Dance with me."

CHAPTER 2

The Dance

"**D**ANCE WITH ME."

The words cut through the noise of the crowd. Not loud or demanding. Just steady, like he knew I'd hear him.

I look up, startled, wiping sweat from my forehead with my handkerchief.

He's a stranger, distinctly taller than most people in the room. He's broad-shouldered, hair swept back from his face and tied neatly, face too angular and sharp-featured to be handsome. A scar cuts across his left cheek.

He's dressed too plainly to be one of Kuya's investors, too clean to be one of the neighborhood kids, too casual to be working at one of the offices nearby. It's just a plain black shirt over some dark jeans.

I should laugh, tell him no. But something in his dark eyes holds me still. Something deep and unspoken. I feel like they've been on me all night.

And maybe I like that.

So I nod.

His hand closes around mine. It's large and calloused, his grip warm and certain. My pulse jumps.

He draws me into the open space where couples sway to Rivermaya. His other hand settles at my waist, steady, anchoring me in the crush of the crowd.

My body tenses, then softens as he guides me. He's close, close enough that I can feel the heat of him through my sweaty shirt, close enough that his chest brushes mine when we change tempo or angles.

"What's your name?" I ask, because I need words to distract myself from how hard my heart is beating.

"Jace." His voice is deep, slightly raspy at the edges. I imagine it whispering my name, and heat rushes to my face.

"Jace…" I repeat, trying it out. It fits. Strong, short, and dangerous. "I'm Lara."

"I know." His mouth almost curves, like he's smiling at some private joke.

He doesn't smell like anyone else here—not beer, not sweat, not even cologne. Just rain and smoke and something clean that clings to my skin when I breathe him in.

"You don't look like someone who hangs out at coffee shop launches," I murmur.

"First time." His gaze never leaves mine. "Worth it."

"Well, that's nice to hear," I say. "You should visit more often. Support local businesses."

"Maybe I should," he answers softly. "If I get to see you like this."

I blush again, swallowing as I look away.

He doesn't say anything, but his hand on my waist digs a little deeper into the fabric of my shirt, the heat seeping into my skin underneath.

The song is ending.

I don't want it to.

He leans in, close enough that his breath brushes my ear. "Thank you for the dance. Goodnight, Lara."

And then he's gone.

He just lets me go, as if the moment never mattered, and disappears into the night.

I stand frozen in the middle of the crowd, breathless, my skin tingling where he touched it, my heart still racing like I've just stepped off the rooftop of a skyscraper.

Whatever the hell that was…

I'm not walking away from it unchanged.

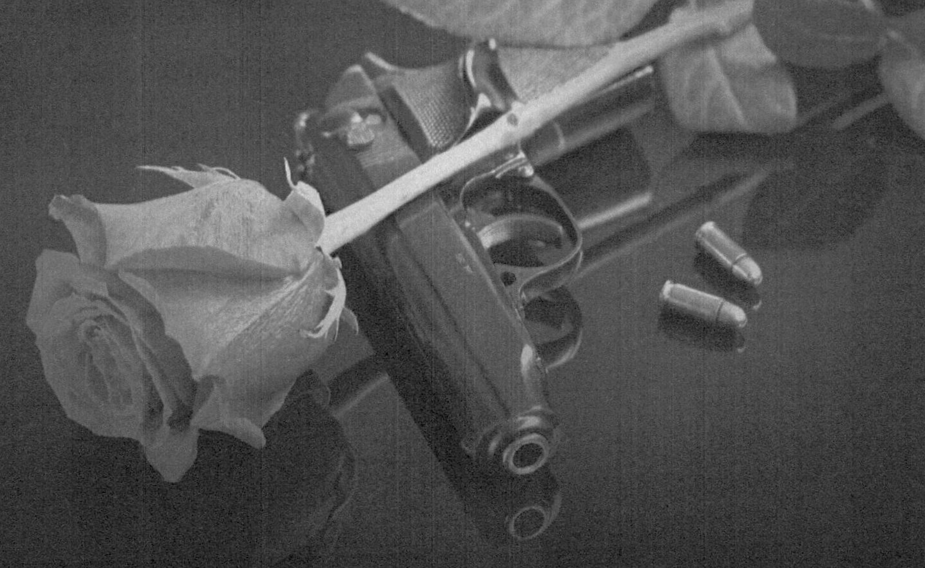

CHAPTER 3

The Job

THE BAR SMELLS OF STALE GIN AND WET ASHTRAYS. I don't remember how many times I've been here before, but I know it's always to pick up my end of a contract. My handler likes the place because no one really asks too many questions.

I sit in the corner booth, shadowed and waiting. The woman arrives late—sharp cream suit, a sharper humorless smile, the kind that says she's paid to make problems vanish. She slides a folder across the table without bothering with pleasantries. This will be my third job with their party.

"Jace," she says, voice smooth. "This one's important. A Congressman's daughter. Leverage. Let's just say we want the old man to get off his high horse."

I don't touch the folder yet. I just listen.

"The girl's visible. Loved by the press. Always on her brother's arm at these little…projects of his. They're trying to build a business empire together, coffee shops and restaurants. A cheap concept, but it makes them accessible, relatable. People like them. Her more so. She's not the usual spoiled rich girl who posts pictures of expensive vacations on social media. She's a college student. All that."

I nod, not saying anything. Politicians don't want their kids to be liked. They want them to be untouchable, just like them. For when the time comes.

"The job is clean," she continues. "Grab her. Hold her. We'll take care of the rest. Price is double your previous fee. We don't want anyone to see or suspect anything. So we got the best in the business for this sort of thing."

I flip the folder open. Photos slide out.

Lara Bienvenides. Up close, in profile, laughing with her brother in front of a coffee cart at Glorietta. Another shot, her in a light dress at some ribbon-cutting event. She looks a bit younger in it.

But it's the same angel of a woman from the party.

Her eyes are just as I remember. Wide, bright, and alive.

I shut the folder before the woman sees too much in my face.

"I'll do it," I say.

"Fifty percent will be wired within the hour," she confirms.

"Make it sixty. I'll let you know when it's time for pick-up." My voice doesn't falter, though my chest feels tight.

She looks at me for a moment, then nods.

"Fine. We'll wait for your call."

In daylight, the coffee shop is small, squeezed between a pawnshop and a convenience store, its new signboard still smelling of paint. Inside, the tables are crowded with students and call center kids nursing cups of cheap caffeine like it's holy water.

I step up to the counter. The menu is handwritten on kraft paper. *Matapang Brew, Puyat Latte, 2AM Americano.*

And then I see her.

She's behind the counter, apron tied around her waist, sleeves rolled up like before. Her thick black hair is in a loose pile at the top of her head. Her skin looks dewy in the soft lights of the shop.

Her brother is in the back arguing with a supplier, and she's running the register herself.

She glances up, and the moment her eyes lock on mine, something clicks into place. Recognition. And wariness. Maybe something else.

For a heartbeat, neither of us speaks.

Then I clear my throat. "Black coffee, please."

She blinks, nods quickly, and turns to pour. The small act—her fingers steady, her hair falling into her face, the steam curling between us—feels louder than the busy chatter of the whole shop.

When she sets the paper cup down between us, our hands almost touch.

"You came back," she says softly.

I wrap my hand around the cup, holding onto the heat. "I said I would. Worth it."

Her lips part, and I see the faintest trace of a smile before she catches herself and looks away.

I turn away without another word, the coffee burning down my throat as I drink it to hide my face.

For the first time in years, the contract feels heavier than the gun under my shirt.

CHAPTER 4

The Walk

THE SHOP IS BUSY FOR ANOTHER HOUR OR SO—students bent over their laptops, workers laughing too loudly over greasy plates of fries and sliders, young couples huddled next to each other sharing brownies and carrot cake.

They're the kind of people my brother says we're here for. Affordable coffee and food, decent Wi-Fi, and no one kicking you out if you sit too long.

By the end of my shift, I'm tired. I take off my apron as I say goodbye to the baristas coming in for the night shift. I grab my bag and phone, notebook tucked under my arm for quick reviews during breaks.

I push open the side door, and stop.

He's there.

Jace leans against the lamppost outside the staff entrance, one hand shoved into his jeans pocket, the other loose at his side.

"Hi," I say, a little awkwardly, throat tight. "Waiting for someone?"

"For you," he says simply, as if it explains everything.

I stare at him. "Why?"

"It's late," he says. "I'll walk you wherever you need to go. Or wait until you get a ride."

Something in me wants to argue, to say I can look after myself, to ask what kind of man waits outside a coffee shop for a girl he barely knows. Besides, I know how to handle myself. My father had made sure of that, since Luke and I were kids.

But the truth is, his presence doesn't feel wrong. It feels…protective. Maybe he's already claimed a right to be here, without me knowing.

"I don't need a ride," I tell him as we fall into step together. "I live just a few blocks away. Small apartment. Right next to my brother's. He makes sure I stay in school even with the business. I've got an exam tomorrow."

"You still study?" His gaze flicks to my face curiously.

"Of course I do. Accountancy, actually. I'm not letting Luke carry everything on his back." I hug the notebook tighter to my chest. "He's building something. And I want to be part of it, properly, as a partner in the business. What about you?"

He shrugs. "Computers. A little bit of this and that.

Mostly contracts. Never got to finish college, but I get by. I live a few blocks out."

I sneak glances at him. The way the streetlamp hits the sharp lines of his face. The scar half-hidden in the shadows. The way he carries himself—graceful yet quiet, every movement measured.

I can't even tell how old he is. He could easily be twenty-five or forty-five.

Jace doesn't say much as we make our way through the streets, but he doesn't need to. He walks close, his stride steady, like he's watching every shadow we pass.

He's not like anyone I know. He's not like anyone I should ever get close to.

And still, something in me wants to.

We stop at my gate. I should thank him, say goodnight, and go inside.

But instead, I look up at him and the words tumble out on their own. "You didn't have to walk me home."

"I did," he replies, the same way he did earlier.

I don't think.

I put a hand on his shoulder, to make him lean down. Then I rise on my toes and press my lips softly to his. Hesitant but quick, before my courage vanishes.

His breath catches, and I feel the smallest tension in him, as if he might pull me back in for more.

But he doesn't. He lets me have this one reckless choice.

I step away, cheeks hot, heart thundering. "Goodnight, Jace."

I slip inside the building, heart still racing, but I can't quite let it end. The kiss still burns on my lips. The warmth of him still clings to my skin.

So I walk to the small window by my desk and push the curtain aside.

He's still there.

Standing under the lamplight, shoulders squared like he belongs to the night itself. He doesn't move. Then, as if feeling my eyes on him, he looks up straight at my window, and catches me watching.

Heat floods my face and neck. But instead of hiding, I lift my hand and give him a wave.

For a moment, nothing. Then he raises his hand in return. Not playful, not shy—but steady, sure, a silent pact I know but don't understand.

It makes me smile anyway. My chest feels too full, like something new is blooming there, fragile but real.

I lower my hand, letting the curtain fall back into place.

On the street below, I know he's still standing there, still looking.

And I stand in my quiet little room, smiling into the shadows, already falling.

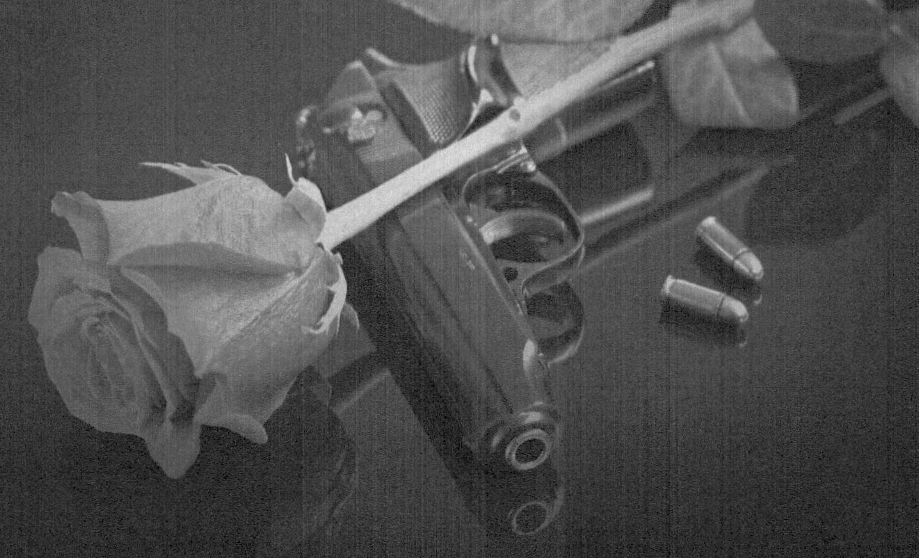

CHAPTER 5

The Night

STAY UNTIL HER SHIFT ENDS.

I listen to the hum of the espresso machine, the sound of chairs scraping against tiles, and the voices of the students and call center kids as they drift out into the night. And still I sit, nursing a coffee gone cold, just to watch her.

Lara moves from table to table, clearing cups and plates. She hums under her breath, absentminded, something soft and tuneless.

She shouldn't be here, in this world where shadows like mine exist. She should belong to the light, where humming and laughter mean something.

Finally, she looks up and sees me still sitting there. Her eyes widen a little. "Jace. You're still here?"

I shrug. "Needed to see how you survived."

Her smile blooms instantly. The sight feels like a full round shot into my chest.

"The exams? Brutal. But I think I passed. Numbers never liked me, but I'm patient with them. Something's gonna give eventually, right?"

"Passing's enough." I lean forward, elbows on the table. "Your brother will be proud."

She tilts her head, studying me like she doesn't quite understand me. "You actually remembered I had exams."

"Of course I did."

Something flickers in her eyes. As if she's not used to people noticing, not like this. She tucks a strand of hair behind her ear, looking flustered, and murmurs, "Most people don't pay attention like that."

I try to smile. As best as I could. "I'm not most people."

She smiles back a little. "No. You're not."

She looks at me for a few more moments before she turns away to finish cleaning up. I watch her pull out her white handkerchief from her pocket and use it to pat away the beads of sweat clinging to her slender neck.

I have never seen something so innocent, yet so erotic.

Fuck it all.

I should leave. I should end it here. But instead, I wait for her to finish up, then walk beside her into the night.

The streets are quiet, pools of yellow light stretching under the lampposts. A stray dog barks, a tricycle rattles past. When she looks at me, her eyes are tired, but soft, almost gentle.

"You don't have to keep walking me home, Jace. I'm used to this neighborhood."

"I know."

"Then why?"

"Because it's late." I glance at her, voice low. "And I'd rather it be me here than someone else."

She slows, just a fraction, as if the words caught her off guard. "You make it sound like the streets are dangerous."

"They are," I say simply.

She studies me, her eyes trying to see beneath the shadows I wear.

"Not when you're around," she replies.

Silence stretches between us. Every step toward her building feels like another step toward the edge of a cliff I can't stop myself from walking off.

At her gate, she stops, turning to me. The lamplight paints her in gold.

She's nervous. I can see it in the way her fingers tighten on the straps of her bag, in the way her breath catches, but she doesn't look away.

"Jace..." Her voice is barely above a whisper. "You're...very different."

I don't ask what she means. I don't want to hear it.

And then she pulls me down by the shirt and kisses me.

It's soft and tentative at first, but it lingers, her hand

brushing lightly against my chest. I feel her heart pounding as fast as mine. When she pulls back, her eyes are shining.

"You're a good man," she says softly.

The words cut through me, raw and merciless. I want to tell her the truth, that I'm anything but, that I'm the danger she doesn't see.

But my voice betrays me. "Don't say that."

"Why not?" she asks gently, almost smiling. "It's true. You look out for me. You don't even realize it, but you do."

Then she reaches up, her fingers lightly tracing over the scar on my cheek.

"You're very special," she says.

I can't breathe.

She doesn't know.

Her hand grazes mine as she lowers it and steps back toward her gate. "Goodnight, Jace."

And just like that, she's gone, door closing softly behind her, leaving me outside with my shadows and her words seared into my chest.

You're a good man. You're very special.

Just like the night before, I look up to see her standing by the window. She waves to me, a smile on her face.

I wave back.

Then I watch her draw the curtains. I don't move.

I stand there long after the lights in her apartment go dark.

And for the first time in years, I hate myself for the job I already agreed to.

I tell myself not to come.

I tell myself to let her walk home alone tonight, to break the pattern before it becomes something I can't undo.

But I'm here anyway, across the street from where I can see her.

Inside the coffee shop, I see her moving, wiping down a table as she talks to the men coming in for the new shift, stretching her arms like she's already half-asleep.

She's humming again. She doesn't know I hear her through glass, that I carry the sound with me into my dreams.

My chest aches. She waved at me. Smiled at me like I was hers to trust. And today, for hours, I thought about that smile. About her lips pressing to mine at the gate, soft and certain, calling me a good man, telling me I'm someone special.

I almost believed her.

Almost.

Then I remembered the file waiting in my room. Her photo clipped to the top. The promise I made to the woman who pays me to finish this.

And the truth—that nothing about me is good.

The side entrance door opens. Lara steps out, bag slung across her body. She pauses for a moment, glancing down the street.

She's looking for me. I see it in the way her eyes linger on the shadows, the faint crease of disappointment when she thinks I'm not there.

God. She wanted me here.

She starts walking. Her footsteps echo against the quiet pavement. I fall into step behind her, silent as I've been trained to be, my body a shadow among shadows.

Three blocks. Then two. My throat is dry.

I should let her go. I should vanish into the dark and forget her name.

I should let the job go.

But my feet move faster.

"Jace?" Her voice is uncertain when I finally step into the spill of the streetlight. She's not afraid. Not yet. She even smiles, faint and relieved. "I thought you weren't coming tonight."

My stomach twists. She doesn't know. She never saw the predator standing in the place of her protector.

I don't answer. I can't. I just reach into my pocket, feel the pouch of dust warm against my palm.

Her smile falters. "What's wrong?"

I step closer. Too close. The scent of coffee and her own cologne clings to her, now dangerously familiar.

"I'm sorry, Lara," I say. "Forgive me."

She opens her mouth to speak, but then I break the pouch, golden powder spilling into the night air.

She gasps, tries to push past me, but her body falters. "Jace…what are you—"

I catch her before she hits the ground. Her head falls against my chest, her lashes fluttering once before the darkness takes her.

I hold her tighter than I should. Too tight for someone who's only a job.

My heart slams against my ribs. She weighs nothing, but carrying her feels like bearing the whole world.

You're very special.

Her words echo in my skull.

You're a good man.

No. I'm not.

I lift her into my arms and disappear into the waiting shadows.

The water scalds my skin, but it isn't enough.

I turn the knob hotter, let it burn across my scar, down my chest, over the hands that carried her here. The sting is better than the cold inside me. Better than thinking about the way she said my name before the darkness closed around her.

Steam fills the bathroom, but it doesn't scrub me clean. The powder dust still clings to my conscience. The lie still rings in my ears.

You're very special. You're a good man.

I press my forehead to the tiles and breathe hard. If she knew who hired me, if she knew why, she'd spit at me, claw at me, even fight until she bled.

And yet she smiled at me. She kissed me. She waved from her window.

She believed in a man who never existed.

I twist the knobs off and step out, water trailing down my back, pooling on the tiles. I dry myself quickly, pull on a black shirt and joggers.

No mask now. No gun. Just me. The man in the shadows.

When I open the bathroom door, the room is hushed except for the low hum of the air-conditioner.

She's still asleep.

Lara lies curled on the bed, small beneath the weight of the hotel blanket, her long hair loose and spilled across the pillow. Her breathing is steady, lips parted slightly, face softened into something that feels too pure for the world she's been dragged into.

For a moment, I just stand there. Watching her. Listening to her breathe.

She looks peaceful.

I hate myself for knowing that peace will shatter in a few hours, when I take her to the rooftop. When the client arrives at dawn.

I drag a chair to the far side of the bed, lower myself onto it. My arms rest heavy on my knees, fingers knotting together as if they could hold me in place.

It should be easy. A job's a job. I've done worse.

But I can't stop staring at her. At the girl who called me good. At the girl who kissed me twice, and meant it.

Dawn is coming.

And I don't know if I have the strength to hand her over.

CHAPTER 6

The Fall

SOMETHING THROBS AT THE BACK OF MY SKULL, DULL and insistent, pulling me up from the dark.

Flashes come back in pieces.

The street. A scarred face. A voice low in my ear.

The sudden blackness.

I open my eyes.

The room is half-dark, curtains drawn, the ceiling broken by restless shadows. A blanket covers me. The mattress beneath me is soft, molding to my body as though I belong here.

I don't.

My pulse spikes. I push the blanket aside, panic scraping raw against my throat. I'm still in my clothes. The white shirt and denim skirt are both intact, a little rumpled, still smelling faintly of coffee. Nothing has been taken from me but time.

Where am I?

The street. The dust.

Jace.

A trap.

My breath hitches as I force myself upright. My body aches, nerves buzzing from whatever he used.

I can get through this.

I see something shift in the corner of the strange room. And I freeze.

He's there, standing at the foot of the bed.

Jace.

Even the shadows can't hide him. His dark eyes are unblinking, and the scar cuts a brutal line across his face. His hair falls loose, framing a jaw too sharp, too merciless.

"You." My voice is nothing but a hoarse whisper, but it fills the silence like a scream. "How could you do this? HOW?"

His eyes flicker. Surprise? Regret? I don't know.

My hand closes around the nearest thing I can reach. It's a glass lamp on the bedside table. I yank the plug free.

And before I can think, it's flying through the air.

He moves fast, but not fast enough. The lamp shatters against the wall beside him, shards spraying out like stars. One cuts across his right side. Blood blooms red against his forearm.

He curses low under his breath, clutching the wound.

I don't wait. I run out the nearest exit I can see.

I find myself on the balcony, wrapped in the heavy night air.

Wind slaps at me, whipping my hair across my face. My chest heaves. I glance down. Endless city lights blur into dizzying streams of yellow and red.

It's too far, too high. If I jump, it's to my death.

Behind me, I hear footsteps.

He's coming.

I spin, throwing myself into a stance I've learned from Karate lessons our parents made me take since I was four. My body trembles, but I bare my teeth anyway.

"Get the fuck away from me, you bastard."

He doesn't answer. His eyes are unreadable, his steps deliberate, corralling me like prey.

I strike first. A kick to the midsection, enough to give me space to run past him. But he dodges it. His counter lands, palm to ribs, slamming the air from my lungs.

Pain cracks through me, and I stumble back.

The railing never catches me.

Only air. Only the plunge.

The world is a smear of black and neon and the howl of wind. I scream until my throat tears.

And then…

Impact. Not with the ground, but with him.

An arm locks around my waist, iron and heat. The rope bites above us, our single lifeline as the city spins below.

My scream dies into a gasp.

"Let me go," I choke out, but it's weak, almost pitiful.

"No." His voice is rough and harsh in my ear. "I can't."

I turn my head just enough to see his face.

The mask of shadows is gone. Only his eyes remain, burning and determined.

They're not the eyes of a monster. They're the eyes of a man bleeding.

A drop hits my cheek, warm and metallic.

Blood.

His blood. From the arm that holds the rope.

From the wound I gave him.

And still he holds.

We rise, inch by inch, until the railing meets us again. He shoves me over it. My legs shake as they find the solid surface of the balcony.

I want to run. But I don't.

He hauls himself after me, landing in a heap. His shirt is soaked, crimson smearing on his skin, his breath ragged.

We stare at each other, silence heavy as the night. He doesn't move. Doesn't reach for me. Just waits.

I could run. I should.

I kneel in front of him instead. "You're hurt."

His eyes flash in the shadows. "What are you doing?"

My handkerchief is already in my hands, trembling as I press it to his forearm. I knot it tight, clumsy but firm. Blood seeps through anyway. My throat aches. "That will help with the bleeding…for now."

When I look up, he's closer than I expected. Too close.

Heat radiates off him, his gaze steady, as steady as the first time I looked into those eyes.

I should hate him. He kidnapped me. He dragged me into this nightmare. But my pulse won't calm, not with his heat seeping into me, not with his eyes dragging me under like tides I can't fight.

His face is inches from mine. His hand brushes my jaw, his thumb grazing my skin like he has every right to. I should recoil. Instead, I shiver.

"Why?" I breathe.

"Because I can't stop," he says. "I can't let go."

Then his mouth claims mine.

The kiss is fire and steel, a clash of everything I should refuse and everything I can't resist. My hands curl into his shirt, pulling him closer, tasting blood and salt and him.

His tongue slides against mine, rough and starving, and I melt into him even as every nerve in me screams danger.

Everything else falls away—the city, the balcony, even the fear. My body betrays me completely, molding against his as though it's been waiting for this.

He drags me onto his lap, his thighs like iron beneath me, his chest hard and hot against mine. The cloth I tied around his forearm is already soaked, blood seeping warm through the fabric, but still his grip is unyielding. One hand digs in my hair, jerking my head back so he can take my mouth deeper, his tongue sliding hungrily against mine.

I moan into him. His other hand finds my hip, then my waist, then lower—gripping, squeezing, dragging me flush against him so I can feel every inch of his arousal pressing against the thin barrier of my skirt.

"Jace," I gasp against his lips, the word breaking.

"You feel that?" he growls, grinding me against him. "You do this to me, Lara. Every single time. That's why."

I shudder, my nails digging into his shoulders, my body rocking helplessly against his. Heat blooms everywhere, consuming and overwhelming.

I should fight. I should pull away. But instead I move with him, straddling him more firmly, my thighs opening over his lap as if my body's already chosen for me.

His hand slips beneath the hem of my skirt, fingers brushing the bare skin of my thigh. I gasp and jolt, but his grip on my hair keeps me right where he wants me.

"Say it," he demands, his breath burning against my mouth. "Say you want this."

"I… I shouldn't…"

"Say it." His fingers skim higher, knuckles grazing the damp fabric of my panties.

A strangled whimper escapes me. "I want you."

He curses harshly, then his mouth is on mine again. His hand presses harder against me through the thin cotton, rubbing slow circles that make my whole body arch into him. My hips grind helplessly against his, chasing the friction, and his groan rumbles through both of us like thunder.

"Goddamn it, Lara," he rasps, biting my lip hard enough to sting. "You'll destroy me."

I'm already destroyed. My body trembles, my thighs

shaking as he pushes me closer, closer, until the tension inside me snaps. Pleasure crashes through me, sharp and shattering, and I cry out against his mouth, my release spilling against his fingers.

He holds me through it, murmuring my name, his hand bruising on my hip. And even when the trembling subsides, he doesn't let go. He just pulls me tighter against him, grinding me against his hardness like he can't bear to stop.

I lean close, lips brushing his ear. "Let me give you this too."

His eyes widen, before he growls something low in his throat. His grip loosens just enough for me to slide down, my hand trailing over his chest, his abdomen, until I reach the hardness straining in his pants.

He hisses through his teeth as I palm him firmly, feeling the weight of him hot and pulsing in my hand. His head falls back against the railing, his jaw clenched, a raw sound tearing out of him.

"Lara…"

I stroke him through the fabric, slow at first, then harder, faster, watching him come apart under me. He grabs my wrist like he wants to stop me, but he doesn't. He can't. He's panting now, hips jerking into my hand, his body trembling with need.

I draw closer, mounting him until my hips are just above his thighs. Enough for him to feel that whatever he's feeling, I'm feeling it too.

"Let go, Jace," I whisper into the night. "Let go."

He swears, a guttural sound, before crushing his mouth to mine again. His kiss is frantic, teeth and tongue and desperation, even as his release builds under my hand. When I finally reach inside his waistband and wrap my fingers around him, hot and rigid and slick with need, he shudders violently.

"Fuck…" he groans against my mouth, thrusting into my fist, every muscle in his body drawn tight. I stroke him harder and harder, faster and faster, my other hand tangled in his hair, until he breaks.

His release spills hot across my hand, across his skin, and he buries his face in my neck with a hoarse cry, clutching me like I'm the only thing keeping him alive.

For a moment, it feels like I am.

When his breathing finally slows, when the tremors ease, he cups my face in his hand. I can feel the rope burns on his palm. His eyes are molten, tortured, and tender all at once. He kisses me softly this time, a contrast so sharp it hurts.

And I know…we are not done.

Not even close.

I know what he wants. I know what *I* want.

For one wild, terrifying second, I want him to take me right here, on the balcony, under the stars with the city lights watching.

I'm still shaking when he kisses me again, his chest heaving. His hands are trembling as they find my cheeks, blood from his wound slick and sticky against my skin.

"I don't want to run," I say against his mouth.

"If I keep you," he rasps brokenly, fiercely, "I destroy you."

The words should terrify me. Instead, they break me open.

Because even as he says it, he goes hard beneath me, throbbing against the soaked cotton of my panties, his body trembling with the effort to hold back.

I can't let him.

I kiss the corner of his mouth, tasting salt and blood and pain.

And I say the words.

"Then destroy me."

CHAPTER 7

The Dawn

SOMETHING INSIDE ME SNAPS.

I drag her against the cold concrete of the balcony, my hands rough, my body trembling with the kind of hunger I've buried since the moment I laid eyes on her.

The city is a blur below us, nothing but lights and noise. Here, it's only her. Her breath shudders into my mouth as I claim her lips, as if she's always been mine. I yank her skirt up, my hand pulling down the thin scrap of her soaked panties.

I stop for a moment. Not out of mercy, but because I feel her trembling, not just from fear.

I slide my fingers over her heat, testing and coaxing.

She's wet.

The realization nearly undoes me. So I do the only thing I could.

I lift her leg, nearly tearing her skirt in half, and bury my mouth in her. She tastes like cream, sweet and a little sticky, as my tongue lap at the juices from her earlier climax.

"Jace," she gasps, pulling at my hair with both hands, her hips jerking closer to my face.

I don't answer. Using my uninjured arm, I reach for her breasts under the cover of her shirt and bra, fingers stroking the nipples as my lips devour the soaking spot between her legs.

"I know, baby," I say against her thigh. "I know. You're ready for me."

"Jace," she says again, her knees bending over my shoulders as she writhes beneath me.

I slide up, covering her body with mine. It doesn't take long for me to lower the joggers, to free myself from the briefs completely. She moans as she pulls my shirt off, her teeth dragging across the bare skin of my chest, her hands digging into my arms, drawing more blood from the wound she'd given me.

And I'm above her, a breath away from making her completely mine.

"Tell me no, Lara," I rasp against her throat, my teeth scraping her skin. "I'll let you go. I promise."

One word could save her.

One word would save me.

"I won't," she says against my lips, then she drags her mouth to my scar, her tongue flicking out to trace it. "Never."

That single word breaks me. I push inside her, and the world explodes.

She gasps, her body so tight. Too tight.

My chest seizes when I realize.

She's untouched. Pure. I'm the first.

"Lara," I groan, my lips finding hers again. "God, you'll break me."

Her nails dig into my back, and I groan louder, half in agony, half in need. I can't stop. I move inside her, slow at first, then harder, deeper, claiming her in every way I know how.

She arches into me, tears glinting at the corners of her eyes, pain and pleasure tangled together.

"You'll destroy me, baby," I growl, kissing her hard, my hips driving her against the concrete until I feel it almost crack.

"Oh, god…Jace!" Her voice breaks on my name. "Don't stop. Please, don't stop—"

Her plea undoes whatever control I had left. I take her brutally, but my hand cradles her face, my mouth drinks every cry she makes. I move faster and faster, until I feel her clench around me, her scream muffled against my lips.

I spill into her with a ragged, broken cry, every drop of me claiming her. I clutch her as if letting go means death.

For one blistering moment, we're one. Flesh and soul and shadow.

When it ends, I collapse against her, our sweat and my blood between us.

Her scent clings to me. Her heartbeat thunders against

my chest, wild and alive. And in that moment, I know the truth I've fought to deny since the beginning.

I love her.

God help me, I love her.

"I should never have touched you," I say, pressing my lips to her soaked hair.

Her hand cups my jaw, her eyes steady despite what I've made of her. "But you did. And I'll never regret it."

I kiss her once more. It's soft and reverent, because it's the last time I'll ever be allowed to. Then I pull away, the shadows closing back around me like a noose.

"Your bag's in the closet. Take my jacket if you want to."

She stares at me. "What are you talking about?"

I don't answer at first. Even as I stand before her bleeding, heart torn open, I help her back into her clothes. I put my arms around her waist and pull her up. I press my lips to her forehead, running my hand through her hair.

I know. I'll never get to touch her like this again.

"Run, Lara," I say softly. "This is the last mercy I have left."

She doesn't move.

"Jace…"

I turn away. "I promised I'll let you go."

Then I walk into the room and sit on the same chair at the foot of the bed.

She stumbles in after me, still wobbly on her feet. It doesn't take long for her to find her things. She slides my jacket on, the fabric swallowing her smaller frame.

She looks at me for the last time, reaching for the doorknob.

"I don't know what to say," she says, her voice small.

I smile at her. "You never had to say anything. Goodbye, Lara."

She doesn't answer.

In a breath, she's gone. Her hair loose, her skirt torn, my blood still drying on her skin.

I watch her from the balcony.

She reaches the street without incident, and mercifully manages to hail a taxi.

I should feel empty. Instead, I feel alive for the first time in years.

"Lara," I whisper into the night, her name torn out of me like prayer.

Like damnation.

I could chase her. I could take her back. I could burn the world down and keep her. I could wage war and win against impossible odds.

I could do it all for her.

But I don't.

Because if I love her at all, I have to let her go.

So I sink into the shadows again, bloodied and haunted, with nothing left but the taste of her on my lips and the fire she's branded into my heart.

And I wait for dawn to come.

FLOWERS FOR THE DEAD

CHAPTER 1

The Daisy and the Lily

I DON'T KNOW HIS NAME.

But every time I pass the plaza near the old church, he's there. Always kneeling in the soil, sleeves rolled up, arms flecked with dirt, hands cradling blooms like they're made of glass. He moves like sunlight, warm and unhurried.

And whenever he sees me, he smiles.

That smile.

I'm supposed to avoid patterns. Routine breeds vulnerability. But I can't stop walking by the plaza since I moved to Arevalo.

Not when I know he'll be there. Not when I know, without fail, he'll leave a flower on the edge of the bench I always pass.

Today, it's a yellow-orange daisy. Bold and bright, almost defiant, against the cloudy day around me.

I pick it up, twirl the stem between my fingers, and keep walking.

❧

I'm a killer.

It's what I do. What I was made for.

The men who raised me never gave me real names. Just contracts and an unbreakable professional code.

To them, I was never even a girl. Or a woman.

I'm just Max.

They carved instinct into my spine, turned emotion into static, and told me love was weakness. I believed them for years.

Then came him.

I don't know why I started watching him. Maybe it was the way he treated every flower like a miracle. Or the way he hummed to himself, off-key and soft.

No mask. No pretenses. Just…peace.

I don't know peace. I know orders, targets, and a hundred ways to make each kill look different from the others.

Still, I make time to pass by.

I reroute. I learn he comes every morning by six. I learn he doesn't use gloves because he says the flowers feel sadness when they're touched by something artificial.

One morning, he catches me watching.

"You always look so sad," he says. The gentleness in his voice hits me like a bullet.

I don't answer. I can't.

He kneels down and pulls a lily from a pallet. "This one's for you. It's for healing."

I stare at the glistening white petals. I don't take it.

He places it on the ground next to my feet before turning back to his work.

For the first time, I don't pick up the flower he gave me.

CHAPTER 2

The Bullet and the Blood

MY LATEST TARGET IS SOMEONE IMPORTANT.

Big businessman with lots of guards. The client is a politician who knows the businessman plans to run for the Congress spot of his district.

The job takes weeks to plan.

And when it goes wrong—when I underestimate their firepower, when the sirens come faster than I expected—I run.

I'm bleeding. My left side burns where the bullet grazed me.

There's nowhere to go. No safehouse close. No contact who won't ask questions.

Except him.

I stumble into the plaza, lungs screaming.

The sun is just rising, casting gold over everything.

And he's there.

He sees me right away. I hear the muffled sound of his spade hitting the dirt.

He rushes to my side, but couldn't reach me on time.

I collapse at his feet.

"Help," I rasp. "Please."

He doesn't ask any questions. He doesn't even say anything. He just lifts me in his arms and carries me to the sidecar of his *pedicab*.

I hear him breathe a little heavier as he pedals away from the plaza.

His house smells like rosemary and soil. There are pots of aloe vera by the window and a bundle of roses on the table. He lays me on his sofa, working silently and efficiently.

He cleans the wound with surprising ease.

As he stitches me up, he says softly, "I'm Ronnie."

"Max," I answer.

Then I pass out.

When I wake, it's night.

He's sitting across from me, reading. When I move, he looks up.

There's no fear or anger or wariness on his face. Just… concern.

"You're lucky," he says. "That bullet could have ended you."

I try to sit up. Pain sears through me. "You should have left me."

He shrugs. "Didn't want to."

"You don't know me."

"I know enough. You're tired. You're alone and sad. And you're not as bad as you think."

He hands me a steaming cup of coffee.

"You could have gotten into trouble," I tell him.

He smiles. "But I didn't."

I stay. I don't mean to, but I do.

A week passes, then two. I sleep on his couch. I start helping him water the plants. He teaches me their names.

I find out he wanted to be a doctor and was even studying in college to be one. He'd dropped out on his third year to look after his sick mother, who ran a small flower garden that had been in her family for generations. His father, who died while he was still in high school, had worked for the church and the convent, doing maintenance and gardening. When his mother passed away five years ago, he simply took on the jobs they left behind.

One night, as I warily look at the rice cooking in the silver pot, I ask, "Why do you keep giving me flowers?"

He gives me a thoughtful look as he unwraps a small parcel of *liempo* he'd bought from the market. He now knows it's my favorite.

"Because you look like someone who's never been given

anything just because," he answers, the words spoken a little too slowly and honestly for my liking.

I could only stare at him.

"And I like seeing your eyes soften," he adds. "You're beautiful, but the first time I gave you that pink rose, your eyes glowed like sunrise. Maybe that's why. You remind me of the light during sunrise."

We don't kiss until the night before I'm supposed to leave.

I haven't told him. I can't. I don't know what this is, what I'm allowed to feel.

But I break when he brushes a soil-stained hand on my cheek and whispers, "You don't have to go, Max."

So I kiss him.

It feels like everything I never let myself want.

That night, we don't sleep.

That night, I let myself believe.

That I could want something, and be wanted back.

CHAPTER 3

The Past and the Sun

BUT I KNOW—THE WORLD ISN'T SOFT.

It's a harsh, judgmental bastard, just like the men who created me.

My past catches up.

They find me in my safehouse near the mangrove reserve.

They tell me to finish the contract. One last target. One last loose end.

After this, they promise me I could leave. Or live. Depends on who says what, really.

I tell them to stuff the money up their asses. I tell them we're quits once the job is done.

But I remember the light in his eyes, the stains on his hands, the warmth of his lips.

So I go back to the plaza at sunrise.

One last time

But no one's there.

I collapse on the bench where he left me flowers.

I can't breathe. Everything hurts.

I close my eyes.

Then…

I feel him.

Arms lifting me.

His voice sounds distant, panicked. "No. No, no, no. You don't get to leave me now."

I try to smile. "You're here. You're finally here."

He cries.

As the world begins to turn black, I say the words.

"Thanks, Ronnie. Love you."

I wake to sun through linen curtains.

To the smell of roses and lilies on the table.

My body hurts, but I'm alive.

He's asleep beside the sofa, bundled in a thin blanket on a mat on the floor next to me. There's dried dirt on the hem of his pants and dark circles under his eyes.

I reach for his soil-stained hand.

"Ronnie?"

He stirs.

His eyes flutter open, then a smile spreads across his face.

"You stayed," I say.

"I told you," he answers. "You're not alone."

He stands up and takes something from the table.

He sinks to his knees before me, and hands me a bright, bold, and defiant daisy.

"I don't think I want to be alone anymore," I tell him.

He nods, then kisses me.

I kiss him back.

"Then you'll never be," he murmurs against my lips.

And for the first time, I believe I'm allowed to stay.

THE FIRE BETWEEN US

CHAPTER 1

The Garden

THE SOUND OF HIS VOICE RIPPLES THROUGH THE QUIET of the garden.

"Viv? Something wrong?"

A shiver runs through me as a gust of wind unsettles the warm summer evening, rustling the bougainvillea and making the air feel suddenly cooler. I close my eyes, lean back in the rocking chair, and let the darkness after sunset press against me like a blanket.

The crickets are singing again, steady and endless, and for a moment I pretend that's all there is—the song, the night, the slow creak of wood beneath me.

The garden has always been my sanctuary. My mother's roses, the scent of soil and old earth, the way shadows bend in the corners but never quite threaten. I've lost hours here, lulled by the familiar.

But tonight the calm feels fragile. Too easily broken.

"Viv?"

His hand lands gently on my arm, warm against my skin.

I open my eyes, push a stray strand of hair from my face, and look at him at last.

Lloyd.

He's been standing here for minutes, maybe more, watching me. Always watching. I wonder if he has guessed what I've been thinking.

How heavy the world feels. Or how brittle I am beneath the surface.

"Hi." My voice comes out softer than I want it to. "I thought you'd be packing for tomorrow's flight."

I stretch slowly, forcing myself into movement, forcing a smile. "It leaves early. And don't think you're skipping my Bon Voyage breakfast. You promised."

He smiles back, his brown eyes glinting like they carry some secret light of their own. Lloyd is handsome in a way that makes people look twice. Dark hair falling around his temples, profile carved in a classic kind of way, a face that would have been at home in an old black-and-white Sampaguita Pictures movie.

And yet, he doesn't belong here. Not in my quiet garden, not in this small town he'd long since outgrown.

"Your breakfast offer is something no sane man would refuse," he teases.

I snort and look away before he can read too much in my expression. "Flatterer."

But he doesn't let it go. He never does.

"What's wrong, Viv?" His voice is gentler now, but more insistent too. "Is something wrong?"

He's more sensitive than I give him credit for. He always has been.

"I haven't eaten much today," I admit, though it's only part of the truth. "Migraine. Takes the appetite away."

He studies me, then slips an arm around my shoulders. I let him, even though the weight of his arm feels both safe and suffocating. "You look pale. Come over to the house. My cousins brought a feast—*lechon, talaba,* the works. I came to see if you'd join us."

I shake my head. "Do you mind if I stay here a while?"

"No. Not at all."

So I rest my head against his shoulder anyway, my body betraying me. For a moment the pain in my skull eases, the scent of his cologne familiar and comforting. He hasn't changed it since college.

Then he clears his throat. "So, Viv."

Something in his tone makes me lift my head. He won't look me in the eyes.

"I hope things are okay with you," he says, too quickly. "You've got to take care of yourself. Tita Roma told me you stay up until dawn, drink coffee like water."

"I work better at night. You know that." My arms fold around me before I even think, shielding myself.

He sighs, then reaches for my hand. I pull it away.

"We're all concerned," he tries again. "Slow down. Don't be too hard on yourself."

"I like my work." My voice takes on an edge. The air between us turns brittle.

"Easy, Viv." He raises his hands like he's surrendering. "I don't want you angry at me for caring about you."

The words slam into me harder than they should.

Caring about you.

I don't let myself believe them. Not when belief could unravel me.

Lloyd has always cared. He's been there with the chocolates on my birthday, the flowers, the ridiculous cartoon cards that made me laugh when no one else could. His sudden return to my life this week has left me off balance, a strange mix of comfort and disquiet. He's been beside me every day, prying open the quiet corners I've built around myself.

"Please," he says. "Don't be mad."

I sigh. I can't fight him, not when he won't fight back. "I'm sorry. Migraines make me cranky."

"Don't apologize." He draws me close again, firmer this time, and presses a kiss against the side of my head.

It's a brotherly gesture. It always has been. We grew up like this. Same street, same schools, our mothers tied by grief and friendship as young widows. He's always been the boy next door, the one who never made me feel small even as he outpaced me in everything else.

I should resent him, but I don't.

Earlier this week, I let him read my draft pitches. He praised them with such sincerity it had left me stunned. Two days later, I was speaking with his editor on the phone, a woman with a kind, smooth voice who told me she was impressed with my samples.

Lloyd had done that. Without asking. Without warning.

Just like that, he had shifted the axis of my world.

But change has always scared me.

Because if he could step in and alter my life so easily, he could just as easily step out again.

And I would be left alone once more, in distance and silence.

CHAPTER 2

The Park

SHE'S ICE.

Not the Vivian I grew up with, the one who laughed too loud and argued with me over nothing just to win. Not the girl who scribbled poems in the margins of our journalism notes. Tonight she's quiet, withdrawn, her words clipped like she's holding them hostage.

And it cuts me.

Because being with her is the only part of this week that has felt real. The reason I traded two big stories, the reason I let my producer's messages go to voicemail, the reason I've ignored the little notes that keep slipping into my inbox.

We know where you live.

Stop writing.

Even the death threats feel distant here, in her garden

in her presence. But Viv, shutting herself off like this…that I can't handle.

I don't want to leave her in this state. Hell, I don't want to leave her at all.

"Why don't we go somewhere," I say, aiming for lightness, like old times. "I don't think I can stomach another bite of *lechon* if I want to run the marathon again."

Her shoulders tense. She pulls away, just enough for me to feel the loss.

Did I say something wrong? Do something? I replay the whole week in my head, every smile she gave me, every silence I filled, and I come up empty.

She hesitates. "Okay. But we need to be back before midnight. You know how our moms are."

Relief sparks in my chest. "The park, then?"

"Okay. Give me a minute. I'll meet you outside."

She slips into the house, leaving me with the echo of her absence.

I head next door, where the cousins are still raising hell. Someone's butchering 'Closer You and I' by Gino Padilla on the videoke, and the table's a mess of pork bones and empty oyster shells.

I grab my mother's car keys. "I'm driving out."

"You mean Lloyd's got a hot night with his girlfriend!" one of my cousins sings into the mic.

Catcalls erupt, whistles following me out the door. My face burns. If Vivian heard that, she'd kill me on the spot.

I make a mental note to ban them all from the house forever.

When I pull up to the gate, there she is. She's changed into jeans and a yellow blouse, hair loose and neatly combed, bag slung over her shoulder. The sight of her steals my breath for a second.

I back the car out quickly before the cousins notice her. She'd hate their attention, and she'd take it out on me.

We're on the coastal road in minutes. The night stretches wide and endless, the sea hidden but near. I glance at her. She's stiff, staring out the window, like she'd rather be anywhere but here.

"Remember when we used to take this car to the *arroz caldo* place?" I ask, trying to catch her smile.

Her lips twitch. "All night café. Too bad it closed down. Nobody makes chicken soup like that anymore."

"I remember," I say. "We'd pool our coins and split a serving."

Finally, she looks at me, her mouth softening into the smallest smile. "And split the egg. Yellow for me, white for you."

I laugh. "Still can't eat the yolk because of you."

The silence that follows isn't heavy. It's companionable, the way it used to be when we were younger, scribbling articles and sharing ice cream straight from the tub. I switch on the radio, soft music filling the car as the lights of the park appear ahead.

We pull into the lot. Couples linger under the lamps,

families are scattered around the playground, but it's quiet enough. I step out, circle the car, open her door. My instinct is to offer my hand, but I stop myself. She flinched earlier, and the last thing I want is to drive her further into herself.

So I just walk ahead, to the wide stone platform by the sea. My chest eases when I hear her footsteps falling into place beside mine.

"I wish the rest of the gang were here," I say, pointing at the swings in the middle of the grassy playground. "Louie, Claire, Faye, Dale—they'd be fighting over those seats already."

Her shoulders loosen, the stiffness ebbing. "They have kids who fight over swings now. I saw Louie and his wife in church last month. Three kids. Can you believe it?"

"Maybe more than a few years have passed," I offer.

"Has it really been that long?" Her voice dips wistfully. "It feels like time moves without me. Like everyone's out there living their lives, and I'm stuck."

Her words stab deep. I stop walking. She does too.

What can I say? What can I do?

Then her hand finds mine, cool and trembling.

"I'm sorry," she whispers. "For ruining your last night here. I must sound so depressing."

"No." I squeeze her hand, fragile in mine. "You sound real."

"My problems aren't your problems."

I turn, really looking at her. The moon paints her in

silver—dark hair framing her face, eyes more expressive and haunting than she realizes, beauty that aches to look at.

My Viv. Always my Viv.

And there's only one truth left in me.

"I could make them mine."

CHAPTER 3

The Sea

MY HEART IS A DRUM IN MY CHEST, SO LOUD I'M SURE he can hear it.

I've been wading through dangerous waters all week. Now it feels like I've stumbled into the deep end, where my feet can't touch the ground.

Someone like Lloyd Mosquera isn't supposed to be here, with me.

He's supposed to be out there, on some high-flying assignment for his column and syndicated show *'Man on Fire,'* his byline in bold, his words sparking outrage and debate across the country.

He's supposed to be untouchable. Larger than life. A man made of fire and ink and distance.

Not this real.

Not standing in front of me, with his eyes burning holes through me.

Not close enough to feel like he could rewrite everything I thought I knew about myself.

"You don't know what you're saying, Lloyd," I say, tearing my hand away and wrapping my arms around myself. It's my armor now, my default defense whenever he makes me feel too much.

It was a mistake coming here. I should have stayed in my garden, safe and small.

But Lloyd never lets go. Not in his writing, not in life.

He rounds on me, his voice raw but still controlled. "The least you could do is give me a little credit, Viv. I do know what I'm talking about sometimes."

"You think you know anything about me?" My voice cracks with the frustration boiling under my ribs. "That somehow, after a week, you could just…fix everything?"

His jaw tightens. He doesn't move, but I feel the force of him like a firestorm barely contained. "Is that what you think I want to do? Change your life? Play the hero?" His voice lowers, hotter and rougher this time. "I couldn't change anyone's life, Viv. Least of all yours."

"Then what do you want?" The tears sting, threatening to spill. I hate them. I hate him for pulling them out of me. "What do you want from me?"

His eyes soften, but his body hums with restraint, like he's one wrong word away from breaking. "I want to be in your life. Not to fix it, not to carry it, but just to be there. When you're stuck. When you can't move."

"Why?" My voice cracks like glass.

"You know why."

The words are a whisper, nearly swallowed by the crash of waves against stone. But I hear them. I feel them.

His gaze says the rest.

And something inside me breaks.

My arms fall to my sides. My knees threaten to give way. Breathing is suddenly impossible, because my chest isn't hollow anymore.

It's full. Too full.

Wonder. Disbelief. Heat. Love.

One spark, and I'm burning.

I don't know who moves first.

Him. Me. Both of us.

All I know is that his mouth is on mine, and I'm lost.

Lloyd kisses like he writes. Unyielding, relentless, pouring everything into it until you're drowning in his truth.

His hand buries itself in my hair, tugging me closer, tilting my head so he can claim me deeper. I gasp, and he swallows it whole, his tongue stroking against mine, setting me on fire.

My hands fist in his shirt, pulling him closer, closer still, until my body is pressed against the solid heat of his. He's all muscle, all strength, the scent of salt and him wrapping around me.

I melt, and he devours.

His mouth trails lower, nipping at the corner of my jaw, down the line of my throat. My head falls back, a shudder ripping through me as his lips burn against my skin.

"I hope you know what you're getting yourself into," I breathe.

His breath is hot against my jugular. "I know exactly where I'm meant to be."

And when he pulls back just enough to look at me, his eyes are molten even in the shadows of the platform.

For years I thought I'd lost him to the bigger world, to the bright lights and dangerous shadows he walked through so easily. I thought he'd left me behind.

But here he is.

And here I am.

My body is fire. My mind is static. Everything inside me says too much.

His hands are in my hair, down my back, gripping my waist with a kind of desperation that makes me feel weak and shaky. He catches me, hauling me against him, and I feel the hard, undeniable press of him through his jeans.

Heat floods me. My body aches for him in a way I can't hide.

"Lloyd," I whisper, half a warning, half a plea.

I know we're hidden from the rest of the world by the seawall, but someone could easily walk down from the park and see us.

"Viv." His voice is ragged, breathless. "Tell me to stop and I will."

But I don't. I can't.

Not even with the risk of getting caught.

Instead, I grab his shirt and tug it up, my fingers skimming hot skin as I push it over his head. The sight of him steals my breath.

Moonlight spills on his broad chest, showing muscles tight from years of carrying the weight of his world. A faint scar slices across his ribs like proof of all the danger he never talks about.

"God," I murmur, tracing it before I can stop myself.

He catches my wrist, eyes blazing. "Not now." And then he's kissing me again, harder, his hands sliding under my blouse, palms burning against my bare skin.

I gasp when his thumbs brush the underside of my breasts, when his mouth leaves mine to trail fire down my throat. "Lloyd…"

"I've always wanted you, Viv," he groans against my skin. "Say you want me too."

"I want you." The words break out of me. "I want you, Lloyd."

That's all it takes.

He pushes me gently back against the cold stone wall of the platform, his mouth finding mine again, his hands tugging at my jeans, fumbling at the button until I help him. The air stings against my skin as he slides them down, his touch following.

My hands dive into his hair, pulling him closer as he presses his hips to mine. The friction makes me cry out, the sound lost in his kiss. He's hard and hot, grinding against me in a way that makes my whole body catch fire.

"Here?" I manage, breathless, half in disbelief.

"Here." His voice is breathless. "I can't wait, Viv. I've waited too long."

His hand slips under my panties, and I arch into him, a cry tearing from my throat as his fingers find me, stroke me, tease me. He knows exactly what he's doing, exactly how to unravel me. I cling to him, gasping, shuddering, my body already spiralling out of control.

And when I'm shaking apart in his arms, he whispers against my lips, "I've got you. Always."

I don't remember how his jeans come off, only the sound of the zipper, the rush of cool air, then the heat of him pressing against me. He looks into my eyes, waiting, trembling as hard as I am.

"Yes," I murmur. "Please."

And then he's inside me, filling me, stretching me until I can't breathe. I clutch his shoulders, nails biting into his skin, and he groans like he's breaking.

He thrusts into me, slow at first, then harder, deeper, each movement sending shockwaves through me. My back arches against the stone, my legs wrap tightly around his hips, pulling him closer and deeper.

"Viv," he gasps, burying his face in my neck. "God, Viv…"

"Don't stop," I beg, meeting him, moving with him, the rhythm building between us until it feels like the whole world has narrowed to his body, his breath, his lips whispering my name.

When release tears through me, it's like the sea itself has risen up to swallow me whole. I cry out his name, trembling, clinging to him as he follows me over the edge, his body shaking, his groan muffled against my skin.

We collapse together, tangled and breathless.

"I hope you know what this means," he says, reaching to trace the curve of my cheek.

"I do," I answer, my body still trembling, my heart still racing. "And I don't care."

Because even if his world is dangerous, even if his shadows follow me now, he knows I've chosen him.

And he's chosen me.

CHAPTER 4

The Shadows

S HE'S STILL TREMBLING WHEN I HOLD HER.

Her breath shudders against my chest, her body soft and pliant in my arms. I swear I could stay like this forever.

The crash of the sea behind us is steady, but all I hear is her heartbeat against mine.

My Viv.

I've wanted her for so long I almost can't believe she's real in my arms, her skin warm, her lips swollen, her scent and sweat all over me.

"I meant it," I say into her hair, my throat tight. "Every word."

Her fingers graze my jaw, and she looks at me like I'm both a miracle and a mistake. "I know."

The undoing in her eyes is enough to break me.

I should stop. I should protect her from this. I should protect her from me.

But I can't. I won't.

Because I know she's always been mine.

She kisses me again, slowly.

"Again," she says, so soft the sound is almost carried away by the wind.

I freeze. "Say what?"

She giggles, then nibbles at my lower lip and whispers, "Don't you dare hold back now, Mosquera."

"Fuck," I growl as she reaches for my cock, already hard again at her touch.

I lay her down on the cold stone. This time I taste every inch of her, mapping her skin with my mouth. Her blouse rides up, baring her to the night air, and I drag my lips down her chest, her ribs, listening to the way she gasps and arches for me.

"Lloyd…" The sound of my name from her lips nearly kills me.

"I wanna taste you, Viv," I rasp, mouth teasing against her skin, until it finally reaches the wetness between her thighs.

I nip and suck, tongue drawing circles, breath tickling the soft, thin hair that carries her scent of roses and dew.

She lets out a strangled cry, hips buckling. *Lloyd. Please.*

I growl against her, my body burning.

Mine.

She's mine now.

When I slide back into her, it's deeper and slower, a claiming as much as a surrender. Her legs tighten around me, and I bury my face against her neck as I move inside her, slow at first, then harder and faster, until we're both coming apart together.

We collapse again, tangled and slick with sweat, her chest rising against mine. I press kisses into her hair, her temple, her mouth, drinking her in to convince myself that everything I ever wanted is now in my arms.

I don't know how long we stay like that. Time feels suspended, caught between her heartbeat and mine.

Eventually, I force myself to say, "We should go."

My chest aches with the words. Leaving feels like cutting a vein open.

She nods reluctantly, and I help her up, smoothing her hair, steadying her when her knees wobble. We laugh quietly at ourselves as we help each other dress, then walk back to the car. My fingers stay twined with hers, unwilling to let go.

But just as I open her door, my phone buzzes. The screen lights up.

Unknown number.

My stomach clenches. I see the message and my jaw locks tight. I shove the phone back into my pocket before she can read the words.

We saw you tonight. Enjoy. We'll be waiting.

"Work?" she asks, her voice soft, almost drowsy.

"Something like that," I mutter, squeezing her hand

before I can stop myself. Then I force a smile I don't feel. "Nothing for you to worry about."

But I do worry. Because the shadows I've been keeping at bay just saw the one thing they can use against me.

I slide behind the wheel. Her hand rests on my thigh, and when I lace my fingers over hers, I swear I'll burn the world before I let anyone touch her.

As we pull away from the park, I know that this is only the beginning.

The beginning of us.

The beginning of whatever storms come with my name.

I can already feel the weight of them pressing closer. Unknown numbers, threats on smuggled notes, whispers from strangers on the street.

They're the kind of enemies who don't stop until they've gutted you.

But tonight I have her hand in mine, her warmth still on my skin, her trust burning in my heart.

I know I'll never let her go. Not this time.

If the world wants a war, it will get one.

Because wherever I go next, whatever shadows rise to meet me, she is coming with me.

MIST AND BLOOD

CHAPTER 1

The Dojo

THE GRAY BUILDING APPEARS AT THE EDGE OF THE shore.

The mist parts, and I see what they call 'the dojo.'

There's no sign, no path.

There is nothing to attract or welcome students.

The place just…exists.

I first heard about it from an old woman who sold me Indian mangoes at the market. She took one glance at the bruise on my cheek and told me to find "the house where the Master lives."

Apparently, he'll teach me to dish it out just as well as I take it.

The other people at the market say the house has always

been here, crouched like a waiting beast between the wet trees and the rocks that cradle the sea.

You don't find it on maps. You don't stumble into it by accident. You arrive when you have nowhere else to go.

I arrive on a Monday.

At least, I think it's Monday, because I'm wearing my school uniform.

My shoes are almost ripped in half. My lip is split from a fight I didn't win. My breath comes shallow, most likely from a bruised rib. My stomach's hollow, but my eyes burn. My wrists are a map of old bruises—some that faded into memory, others still pulsing beneath the skin.

I walk through the early morning fog, my arms wrapped around myself—not for warmth, but for armor. The plain gray walls rise out of the mist like something ancient. The roof is heavy with leaves. The courtyard pools with rain.

And the Master is there.

I don't know his name.

He looks like stone carved into a man—angular face, high cheekbones, narrow jaw, eyes that look like the mist I just walked through. His hair is long and black streaked with silver, tied back like a warrior from a forgotten time.

He watches me. I don't know if he's being kind or cruel or curious.

He's just still.

He even doesn't ask why I'm here.

He just picks up my soiled green backpack full of torn clothes and walks into the dojo.

And I follow.

CHAPTER 2

The Master

LEARN AND SERVE IN SILENCE.

No formal greetings. No initiations. Just days that become weeks that become months.

I don't go to school, but I read the books that fill the shelves in the hallway.

I cook and clean and do laundry. I go to the market in town. He gives me money to buy supplies and pay bills.

I talk to the students and their parents like a model employee.

I sleep in a tiny outhouse at the edge of the property, nestled between groves of coconut trees.

The rest of the time I don't stop training.

He never raises his voice. He doesn't praise or scold.

He exists like gravity. Something I adjust to, something I resist. Something I eventually learn to trust.

When I stumble, he catches me.

When I scream, he lets me.

When I collapse, he waits.

When I get the attacks in the middle of the night, he carries me to the dojo and lets me cry myself to sleep on the mats.

I learn to move with precision. To strike without hesitation. To still my breath until even the rain sounds like rhythm. My fists learn to break brick. My muscles harden. My fire refines itself, no longer wild, but contained and ready.

And at night in my tiny outhouse, my heart racing with echoes of old horrors, I feel him there.

Something near enough to reach.

CHAPTER 3

The Typhoon

THE YEAR'S TYPHOON SEASON IS THE MOST CRUEL YET. The sea winds grow vicious. My bones ache, but I still train in the courtyard barefoot, under the lashing rain, letting the cold needles bite me into clarity.

He passes me sometimes. Our eyes meet, but there are no words.

I've come to crave that between us.

One night, it all changes.

I'm walking back from town, a bag of supplies slung over my shoulder, when I see a figure blocking the gate.

It's the uncle I stopped calling uncle years ago.

He's drunk. Smiling that smile I grew up dreading. The one that always came before the hurt.

"Look at you," he slurs. "All grown up. Think you can hide from me, little rat?"

I don't answer.

His hand reaches out, filthy, groping.

This time, I don't even think.

I break his jaw with the heel of my palm.

My kicks land harder than I ever thought possible. I hear his ribs break.

There is blood on my shoes. His breath stops before mine does.

I call the police on my phone. I give myself up.

The municipal jail is gray and stinking and rusty.

I sit on the wooden bench, my hands still stained red, my knuckles swollen. The guards don't ask questions.

The woman in a miniskirt across from me in the cell looks at me with a respectful nod and asks if she could braid my hair. I say yes.

I don't tell her my story, but she tells me I remind her of her daughter. The one who left her after losing a battle with dengue. We'd be about the same age now, she says. We even have the same texture hair.

I don't cry, but I let her.

I watch the woman doze off. I slide to the floor and lean against the sticky wall, hoping I could at least rest my burning eyes.

Even then all I think of is the dojo. The lashing rain. Him.

It's dawn when the cell door creaks open.

A young officer gestures for me to stand up and get out. The woman next to me is still fast asleep.

I rise to my feet. My whole body shakes.

I see him standing just outside.

He doesn't even look at me, but I know he's there for me.

The only solid and real thing in my life.

The local police chief is shaking his hand, refers to him as "Mr. Villarete."

We walk out of the station together, across the municipal plaza where his multicab is parked. The sky is gray. The wind bites. The world looks damp and worn.

"Did you put towels by the eastern window?" I ask him suddenly.

He shakes his head. "I forgot."

I sigh. "It's okay. I'll mop it when I get home. I—"

"Cassandra." He never calls me by anything other than my real name. He inhales deeply before continuing. "Are you okay?"

I nod, facing him. My breath clouds between us. My voice cracks as I say, "Why did you come?"

He reaches up.

His hand is warm as it brushes my cheek tenderly, carefully.

"Because you fought back," he says.

That's when I kiss him.

Not out of want. Not at first.

Out of everything else. Pain. Loss. The ashes of stolen girlhood, reborn in his care.

But when he kisses me back, it's like a typhoon unravels inside me. It feels like my sorrow has teeth, and his lips are forgiveness.

We spend the night together, on his mats.

I finally call him by his name, "Anthony."

When I wake up the next morning, he is gone.

The dojo is still there, but it is hollow.

He left no note. No goodbye.

Just…absence.

And the mist of him.

CHAPTER 4

The Courtyard

YEARS LATER, I STAND BAREFOOT IN MY COURTYARD.

The gray walls still stand. I repainted them with my own hands.

Children run through the rain-soaked courtyard, laughter ringing off the stone. They swing sticks too big for their arms, shout like they're fighting dragons.

And I let them. Then I will teach them how to be still.

How to breathe. How to rise.

How to rise again after they fall.

I will teach them how to survive without apology.

On my desk, there's a photo. Black and white, grainy with time. It's the only one I have of him.

Eyes like mist. Face like stone. Hands as gentle as the breeze, as strong as the wind.

I trace his face every night. I talk to him often.

But I never saw him again.

But sometimes, when the mist rolls in thick and the ocean before me tastes like salt and promise, I feel him near.

And I smile.

I'll never be alone. I'll never be afraid anymore.

Because I carry him in my bones, in my breath.

In the way I move. In the way I teach.

Because the blood in my veins still remembers the Master that welcomed me home from the mist.

And his kiss that saved me.

ABOUT THE AUTHOR

Shirley Siaton writes edgy and evocative novels and poems. Her worlds are in a deliciously dark cross-section of the romance, neo-noir, action, contemporary, and fantasy genres. Her background in various Asian martial arts inspires a lot of her work.

She has several books of fiction and poetry released since February 2023. Her first book is the free verse collection *Black Cat and other poems. Befallen* (March 2025) is her first full-length novel. She also pens juvenile literature as Shirley Parabia.

She is an award-winning writer, poet, and journalist in English, Filipino, and Hiligaynon. Her essays, short stories, and poems have been published internationally in print and digital media. Her multi-lingual plays have been staged in the Philippines.

Shirley is a black belt in Shotokan Karate and an international certified fitness coach. She has a Master's degree in Public Administration and works in education, wellness, and publishing. Originally from Iloilo City, she lives in the Middle East with her husband and two daughters.

ON THE WEB

Shirley's official website:
shirleysiaton.com

Complete reading guide:
shirley.pub

Subscribe to Shirley's VIP list for free exclusive updates:
newsletter.shirleysiaton.com